Dunc's Doll

OTHER YEARLING BOOKS YOU WILL ENJOY:

THE CASE OF THE DIRTY BIRD, *Gary Paulsen*
THE VOYAGE OF THE *FROG, Gary Paulsen*
CHOCOLATE FEVER, *Robert Kimmel Smith*
JELLY BELLY, *Robert Kimmel Smith*
MOSTLY MICHAEL, *Robert Kimmel Smith*
THE WAR WITH GRANDPA, *Robert Kimmel Smith*
HOW TO EAT FRIED WORMS, *Thomas Rockwell*
HOW TO FIGHT A GIRL, *Thomas Rockwell*
HOW TO GET FABULOUSLY RICH, *Thomas Rockwell*
UPCHUCK SUMMER, *Joel L. Schwartz*

YEARLING BOOKS/YOUNG YEARLINGS/YEARLING CLASSICS are designed especially to entertain and enlighten young people. Patricia Reilly Giff, consultant to this series, received her bachelor's degree from Marymount College and a master's degree in history from St. John's University. She holds a Professional Diploma in Reading and a Doctorate of Humane Letters from Hofstra University. She was a teacher and reading consultant for many years, and is the author of numerous books for young readers.

For a complete listing of all Yearling titles,
write to Dell Readers Service,
P.O. Box 1045, South Holland, IL 60473.

Gary Paulsen

Dunc's Doll

A YEARLING BOOK

Published by
Dell Publishing
a division of
Bantam Doubleday Dell Publishing Group, Inc.
666 Fifth Avenue
New York, New York 10103

If you purchased this book without a cover you should be aware that this book is stolen property. It was reported as "unsold and destroyed" to the publisher and neither the author nor the publisher has received any payment for this "stripped book."

Copyright © 1992 by Gary Paulsen

All rights reserved. No part of this book may be reproduced or transmitted in any form or by any means, electronic or mechanical, including photocopying, recording, or by any information storage and retrieval system, without the written permission of the Publisher, except where permitted by law.

The trademark Yearling® is registered in the U.S. Patent and Trademark Office.

The trademark Dell® is registered in the U.S. Patent and Trademark Office.

ISBN: 0-440-40601-3

Printed in the United States of America

July 1992

10 9 8 7 6 5 4 3 2 1

OPM

Dunc's Doll

Chapter · 1

Duncan—Dunc—Culpepper and Amos Binder were sitting on the bench in Dunc's garage. Dunc's bike crank was loose, and he was taking it apart and tightening it, greasing the bearings carefully as he fit them back into the clean housing, sitting in new grease. He put each steel ball in separately, gently.

Amos was frustrated. "Come on—you'll be all day with that. I want to get down to the mall. We haven't tried that new video game—Splatter Space Defense. It's in high-

1

definition color, and you can actually see pieces of the aliens flying off if you hit them right."

Dunc stopped, looked up. "A job worth doing is worth doing right. It might be ten years before I have to take this crank apart again."

"Ten years?" Amos snorted and picked at a scab on his chin. "I've *never* taken the crank off my bike."

Dunc looked at Amos's bike, leaning against the wall. It looked like a car had been parked on it for a week. "I can see that."

"In ten years," Amos said, "I'll have a car, and Melissa and I will be happily married, and you can come over and teach my kids how to take their cranks apart. But for now, let's get *going*. You want to spend your whole life in a garage?"

But Dunc didn't hurry, and he didn't pay any attention to Amos's pushing. They'd been best friends for as long as he could remember, and for at least that long Amos

2

had been pushing at him. "How did you cut your chin?"

"It happened last night. I was home alone, or thought I was, reading in the tub, and the phone rang. I was certain it was Melissa's ring—it had that sound. You know, that kind of ring she has, followed by another ring?"

Dunc nodded. Amos had been waiting for a call from Melissa as long as he had known Amos. Melissa didn't show any sign that Amos was alive. It was like, Dunc thought, like he was invisible. Like she could read a book through him.

"Well, you know I like to get it on that all-important second ring. So I cleared the tub still wet and naked and hit the hallway and hung a left trying to get to the phone in the front hall." Amos shook his head. "Man, I had it all—my balance was working right, I was in good stride, had some form, and I think I would have made it."

"What happened?" Dunc put the last

ball bearing back into the crank and fit the shaft through the hole. Carefully.

"Mother came home. She'd been doing Welcome Wagon and had three Welcoming ladies with her. They were all by the hall phone."

"Bad," Dunc said, shaking his head, trying not to smile. "Bad style—you naked and all."

Amos nodded. "I tried thinking of an excuse, but I was moving too fast. I did manage a grab at the phone—it was just instinct —and that threw me off, and I hung a foot on the doorjamb. That's"—he took a breath —"when things started to go bad."

"Not until then?"

Amos shrugged. "Well, I was a little embarrassed, but I still hadn't been injured."

"So how did it go bad?"

"I lost it. I was still going at a full run, and I went down. I was so wet I was slippery and I kind of scooted across the carpet on my stomach. Like a dead fish. I hit a dining-room chair headfirst and caught my head between two rungs on the bottom."

"How did you get out?"

"Mother had to grease my hair." Amos sighed. "All in all I had a pretty bad night. You ever try to get dressed with a chair stuck on your head?"

Dunc shook his head and finished tightening the crank. "No—there, it's done. Let's get going—you going to mess around all day?"

Chapter · 2

Pioneer Mall was on the way toward town. Dunc's home was on the outskirts in a development, and it took the two boys just fifteen minutes to bike to the mall.

Out in front there was a large signboard, and they always had something different on the sign—some activity or message.

This time it read:

> "Happy Birthday Carl and
> may you have forty more."

And:

"DOLLS, DOLLS, DOLLS—
antique collections."

"Oh great," Amos said as they pedaled into the parking lot. "Dolls."

"I think they're kind of interesting." Dunc locked his bike in the rack.

"You do? You mean dolls?"

Dunc nodded. "Antique dolls. This collection has dolls that belonged to famous people. There's one that belonged to Charles Dickens's daughter."

"You mean the guy who wrote *A Christmas Carol*?"

Dunc nodded. "Yeah."

"He had a family?"

"Sure—at least, he must have. He had a daughter. They've got her doll in here."

"Well—I'm going to the video arcade. Are you coming?"

Dunc nodded, but he didn't head for the arcade. Once inside the mall he walked toward the end, where the doll collection was on exhibit.

8

"Oh, come on," Amos said. "What if somebody we know sees us?"

Dunc stopped. "Another way to look at it is—what if Melissa sees us? I just saw her down at the other end of the collection."

"You did?" Amos caught up. "She's probably looking for me—wants to know why I didn't answer the phone last night."

"Don't tell her," Dunc said, smiling. "Don't tell anybody."

But Amos wasn't listening. He'd seen Melissa.

Dunc wandered past the dolls. He was looking for the Dickens doll and finally found it at the end of the table. It was in a special glass case with a light on top shining down inside the glass.

It was a doll of a small man in a black suit, wearing a tie and a hat.

"It's called a father doll," the man behind the counter said. He wore a name tag that said *Carruthers*. "Are you interested in dolls?"

Dunc shook his head. "No, not really.

Just this one. I read about it in the newspaper and thought it might be nice to see it."

"The face is hand painted," the man said. He was tall and thin and stooped with a soft smile and a pocket full of felt-tip pens. "And the suit is hand stitched, probably by child labor—which is ironic, isn't it?"

Dunc frowned. "Why?"

"Because Dickens worked hard to end child labor and yet bought a doll that was probably made using children."

The face on the doll was crude, but considering how it was made, it wasn't so bad. "How old is it?"

"I'm not certain—it was probably made in the mid-1850s."

Amos had come up. "She was busy with friends," he said to Dunc's unasked question. "I didn't want to bother her." He looked at the doll. "Ugly, isn't it?"

Carruthers laughed. "Well, maybe. But as you can see in the article, many people think it's lovely."

There was a news clipping taped inside

the case. Amos read the article while Dunc studied the doll.

Amos whistled. "It says the doll is worth fifteen thousand dollars. Is that right?"

Carruthers nodded. "Actually, it's worth considerably more. That article was written fifteen years ago. The worth of the doll might be nearly thirty thousand by now."

"Thirty thousand? And you just show it to people?"

Carruthers nodded again. "The malls pay me enough to keep the collection going. I travel around and show the dolls, and I have a little pension. It's a nice way to live."

"You don't sell them?" Dunc asked.

Carruthers shook his head. "No—I just like to show them. And meet people who are interested in them. There are conventions, and sometimes we trade dolls there. That's how I got the Dickens doll—I traded a doll that had belonged to Martha Jefferson. She was Thomas Jefferson's wife."

Dunc read the article. Amos had moved around to a position where he could watch the end of the mall where he had seen Melissa.

"It says here there have been attempts to steal the dolls," Dunc said. "Does that happen a lot?"

"No." Carruthers smiled. "That's other people's collections. I've never had any trouble at all. I guess I'm just lucky."

"So far," Dunc said.

Within a few weeks, he would wish he'd never said it.

12

Chapter·3

"I figured out how to get rich," Amos said. It was a week after they'd been in the mall and seen the dolls. They were back in Dunc's garage. He was tearing the front end of his bike apart, regreasing the bearings inside the front fork.

"I'm just going to ask people for money," Amos said. "They'll give it to me."

Dunc shook his head. "What makes you think that?"

"Last night my uncle Alfred—the one who picks his feet?—anyway, he was watch-

13

ing one of these television ministers. The guy just looked at the screen and said: 'I feel like somebody is going to send me a thousand dollars. God is telling you, whoever you are, to send me a thousand dollars.' "

"That's different."

"Why? He's just asking, isn't he? Uncle Alfred says people send in millions of dollars to these television ministers and all they do is just ask for it. So that's what I'll do. I'll put an ad in the paper and just ask for money."

Dunc had stopped listening. Always neat —sometimes to the point of driving Amos crazy—Dunc had put newspaper under the bike wheel so he wouldn't spill grease on the garage floor.

A headline in the paper had caught his eye.

" 'Dolls Stolen,' " he read.

"What?" Amos asked.

"There's a story here about some dolls being stolen—oh, no."

"What's the matter?"

Dunc pulled the paper out. "It's that man we met in the mall, that Mr. Carruthers. Somebody broke into his van and stole some of the dolls. The article says the thieves waited until he was away from the van, and they just took four dolls—the ones that were the most valuable."

"That's too bad."

"Yeah. Hmmm . . ." Dunc read some more to himself.

"What do you mean—'hmmm'?" Amos said. "I don't like it when you do that. Last time you made that sound, I wound up losing my eyebrows and couldn't hear right for two months."

"It's just that they don't have any leads. It seems a shame. He had to leave town to get to his next show, and he isn't here to try and find the dolls."

"The police will handle it."

"They said they didn't have any leads."

Amos shook his head. "We were going to

15

take that bike trip next week, remember? You're going to get us all messed up in something to do with dolls. I mean *dolls.*"

"I didn't say we were going to get messed up in anything."

"I know when you make that sound, that *hmmm* sound—I know what that means."

Dunc read on. "It says there's a reward. The American Doll Association is putting up a reward."

"I like my idea for getting rich better. Let's just ask for it."

"Come on," Dunc said. "Let's at least take a look at it. You can't tell."

"But dolls," Amos said. *"Dolls."*

Dunc put the paper down. "The way I figure it, the first thing we have to do is talk to somebody who knows something about dolls—see what they mean to people."

"Dunc, we can't—"

"I figure we go and talk to Melissa."

Amos stopped. "You say there's a reward?"

Dunc nodded.

"That Mr. Carruthers *was* kind of a nice guy, wasn't he?" Amos said. "Well—maybe it won't hurt to take a look at it."

Chapter · 4

"I've had it." Amos stopped his bike. Dead. He watched Dunc pedal away and waited. Finally Dunc stopped and looked back.

"What's the matter?" Dunc asked. It was the middle of the afternoon, a beautiful sunny summer day, and they were biking along a country road just leaving the city.

"This is nuts, that's what's the matter," Amos said. "It's been three days since you saw that dumb newspaper story, and all we've done is run around looking at dolls.

You know what this is doing to our reputation?"

Dunc came back. A car roared by, and he waited for the noise to drop. "Listen—dolls aren't so bad. You played with G.I. Joe dolls and monster dolls, didn't you?"

"That's when I was young. I was just a kid then. This is different, and you know it."

Dunc decided to try another angle. "You got to talk to Melissa, didn't you?"

Amos stared at his friend. "You're kidding, right?"

Dunc shook his head.

"She said hi," Amos said. "And I think she was talking to you when she said it. She looked right through me, and then she talked to you about dolls. Not me. You. For about three minutes. Then she walked away and that was it. For that, you've got me riding my bike all over the city for three days looking at dolls."

Dunc shrugged. "You know that most of an investigation is work, work, work—almost all for nothing. Until you pop a lead."

20

"And that's another thing," Amos said. "You talk like a cop. We're not cops. We're a couple of kids—"

"Who have a chance at a reward," Dunc finished. "Now, come on—we're wasting time."

He turned and started off down the country lane again. Amos held back until Dunc was out of sight around a bend, then he shook his head and biked to catch up.

"Where are we going?" he asked, pedaling alongside Dunc. "I mean, this time?"

"It's a rich man on an estate—his name is Wylendale. He collects all sorts of things. Antiques, art, dolls, guns."

"Guns?" Amos's ears perked up. "This guy has guns? We're going to see somebody who is armed?"

Dunc laughed. "He has old stuff—old guns. That doesn't mean he's bad or anything." He shrugged, his bike weaving slightly with the gesture. "Of course, it doesn't mean he *isn't* bad either. I got his

21

name from Mrs. Dooley—the last woman we talked to."

Amos nodded, remembering. They had been going from one collector to another for the three days that they'd been working on "the case," as Dunc liked to call it.

Yesterday they'd gone to see an old woman named Mrs. Dooley. She collected stuffed animals and dolls, and Dunc had talked to her while Amos looked at all the animals.

"Imagine," he said, riding closer to Dunc, remembering her house, "a special room for a stuffed elephant. A whole elephant."

Dunc nodded. "She said she never killed an animal in her life but was buying them from other collectors so there would be some way to see how they looked when they were extinct."

"Right. That's why she had a stuffed cocker spaniel."

"That was her pet. She told me about it.

22

He died when he got old, and she loved him so much, she had him stuffed."

"Was she a widow?" Amos asked.

"I don't know—why?"

"She might have her husband stuffed in the basement."

"Here we are." Dunc pulled over to the side of the road. "Wow—look at it."

They were facing a large wrought-iron gate with the initial *W* welded in steel rods into the iron.

The gate was held locked by a large steel bar that came in from the side and appeared to be controlled by an electrical motor.

"Friendly, isn't he?" Amos said.

"Oh, maybe he just likes his privacy," Dunc said. "I mean, lots of people have closed gates."

He paused as a shadow appeared at the side of the gate. It moved into the open, and they could see that it was a dog.

A Rottweiler.

He stopped and stared at the boys across the road.

"He's looking at me like I was made of meat," Amos said. "Raw meat."

"Well, that does it," Dunc said.

"Does what?"

"I've got a feeling—this is it. Why would he keep a locked gate and a huge Rottweiler if he didn't want to hide something?"

Chapter · 5

Amos was staring at him.

"Are you out of your mind?"

"Well—it's logical, isn't it?"

The dog still stared at them. It was silent, not even growling. Just staring.

"Look at him," Amos said. "You're about to mess with somebody who keeps a dog that thinks I'm made out of meat."

Dunc nodded. "We'll have to handle it right. This time we can't just sneak in. He probably keeps the dog loose all night. We wouldn't get fifty feet."

"Well, I'm glad we agree on something. So, we'll just drop it all, right? I thought I'd like to live long enough to maybe go to high school."

But Dunc was already riding back the way they had come, lost in thought.

They were in Dunc's room.

Amos looked around the walls. "You've got all new posters in here."

Dunc was looking at a map, and he shook his head. "Not new—they're old. I brought them in here approximately 130 days ago."

Amos stared at him. "You recycled your old posters?"

Dunc nodded. "Visual boredom can stifle the thinking processes. I keep a record on the computer and store the posters in the basement. There's a regular cycle, and I bring in new ones as they come along."

"Why didn't I know this?"

Dunc shrugged. "I don't know—there's lots of things about you that I don't know. It's just one of those things."

26

"What?" Amos asked.

"What, what?"

"What don't you know about me?"

Dunc stood up from his desk and turned to his friend. "Amos, if I knew what I didn't know about you then I would know about it, wouldn't I?"

"You're just trying to confuse the issue."

"It's already confused." Dunc turned back to the map. "Now, look on this plat map."

"What's a plat map?"

"It's a city map of the area we're investigating. See here, there's Wylendale's place."

"Where do you get these things? These maps and things?"

"I borrowed this one from my father. He needs these maps to sell real estate. He's got one for every area in the city, even out into the country. Now look, quit messing around."

Amos leaned over the map.

"See, here's his property. I think it's about six acres—a really big place. But look, look at this road going out the back and winding down along the railroad here. There's a narrow road that runs all along the tracks—it must be for two or three miles—and comes out on the highway."

"So? What's the matter with having a back road?"

"It's where he could ship all the stuff out."

"What stuff?"

"Stolen things. Dolls."

"Oh man, you're stretching now—that's crazy. We see a padlock on the gate and a Rottweiler that thinks I'm meat, and you've got him stealing dolls."

Dunc sighed. "I know. We just don't have enough information. That's why we need to get in there and dig a little. Don't worry, I've got a plan."

"You do?"

Dunc nodded. "No problem. The thing we're after is a doll, right? So all we have to do is pretend we're interested in dolls for some reason."

Amos shook his head. "You're nuts. Two boys come to the place and ask about dolls, and you don't think they'll figure it's a little weird?"

"Well, that's just it," Dunc said. "It won't work if two *boys* come to the gate. You hit it right on the head."

Amos waited.

"It has to be a girl. One of us has to dress up as a girl and fool them."

Amos was up and headed for the door. "Nope—you're nuts. Not me. Not your old friend Amos. Not on your life. Not this time."

Dunc held up his hand. "Did I say it was you? Did I even *hint* that it was you? Nope —I figured to do it myself all along. Even though I'm kind of chunky and stocky and you're built more for it, being thin and all. But no problem."

"Well, all right. Just so you understand."

Dunc shrugged. "I just figured you'd *want* to do it, is all."

"Me? Why would I want to dress up like a girl?"

"Well, not that. But do the disguise. I was sure you'd want to be the one."

"Nope, not this time."

Amos waited, but Dunc didn't say anything further. He waited some more, chewing on his bottom lip.

"All right—why?"

"Why what?"

"Why would I want to be the one to dress up like a girl?"

Dunc smiled. It was the same smile a cat might make just before it nailed a bird. "Well, the news and all. If we get the doll, whoever wears the disguise and goes in to get more information will be a hero. Television will want to talk to him more than the other one—the one who stays back."

Amos waited.

"Well there you are on the news, saving this valuable doll, and who sees it?"

Amos waited.

"Melissa," Dunc said, repeating, "and there you are."

Amos sighed. His shoulders slumped. He nodded. "Right—there I am."

Chapter·6

"Oh, man, this is awful."

Amos was standing in front of a mirror in the hallway of Dunc's house. He was wearing girls' jeans and a sweatshirt too big at the neck so it hung down on one shoulder.

And a blond wig.

Dunc shook his head. "No—it's not too bad. I think we might need some makeup."

"I'll kill you," Amos said, his voice even, flat, "if you so much as *try* to put makeup on me."

"Well, there's something wrong with it."

Amos studied himself in the mirror some more. "I know what it is."

"What?"

"I'm ugly." Amos frowned. "You've got me being ugly."

"What do you mean?"

"Well, just look at me. I'm not a blonde, not at all. And you've got me being a blonde. It just isn't my color."

"Amos . . ."

"Well, really. If I'm going to *be* a girl, I don't want to be an *ugly* one, do I? Doesn't your sister have a brown or black-haired wig?"

Dunc went back into his sister's room and came out with a black-haired wig.

"If she catches us doing this, she's going to kill us," Amos said.

"She's away for the weekend. Here, hold still while I put this on."

Dunc took the blond wig off and put the black-haired wig on.

"How's that?"

Amos straightened it, settled it on his head. "Well, it's better—can't you see the difference? It goes much better with my eyes, don't you think?"

"You're still ugly, if that's what you mean."

"I am not—not as bad as before." Amos turned left and right, looked at his reflection. "See, I look a lot better."

"I was just kidding. Now let's get going." Dunc ran the blond wig back into his sister's room.

As they were going out the front door, they ran into Dunc's mother. She had her arms full of sacks of groceries.

"Hi, Mom," Dunc said.

"Hi, Mrs. Culpepper," Amos said, and was out the door before it closed, ducking under the sacks to get by.

Dunc's mother turned, looked at the closed door for a moment. She started to say something, then changed her mind and walked away, shaking her head.

"It's better," she said, "not to know."

Chapter·7

They looked at the gate.

Dunc had hidden his bike out of sight in some bushes across the road from the gate.

"You go over there and push the bell button next to the gate," Dunc said. "I'll go hide with my bike. When they come, you tell them you're doing a paper on doll collections for a summer school project. You got that?"

Amos nodded. "Of course. We've been over it a couple of hundred times."

They separated, and Dunc went to the

brush across the road. Amos went to the gate. On the side of the gate was a plaque with a push button and Amos pushed the button.

Nothing happened for what seemed a long time.

Then the dog came to the gate. It stood on its back legs, its front feet up on the metal, and looked at Amos, down into Amos's eyes.

Amos turned and looked across the road at where Dunc was hiding, raised his arms, and shrugged. The movement wiggled his wig, and he straightened it. Dunc made a furious motion to Amos to turn around, and he did.

And the dog still stood there, looking down on him.

"He can drip spit on the top of my head," Amos turned and yelled.

"Don't look at me," Dunc yelled.

Then the sound of an engine came from the driveway, and Dunc dropped out of sight.

38

A dark car pulled up to the gate and a tall, thin man stepped from the car.

"What do you want?" he asked.

"My name is Sally Carstairs," Amos said. "I'm doing a paper on doll collections for a summer school project. May I see your collection?" Amos had it memorized perfectly and said it all in one breath.

The tall man looked around, up and down the street, then across the street almost directly at where Dunc was hiding.

"Where are you from?"

"In town," Amos answered. "Some of us —some of the girls were talking about your collection, and I got the assignment. To do a paper. On your dolls. The collection, I mean."

"Just a minute. It's not my collection. I just work here."

"Could you do something about the dog? He's looking at me funny."

"No."

"Thanks, anyway." Amos shot a look

across the road at Dunc but could see nothing.

Dunc was on his stomach by this time, peering through the grass.

The thin man turned to the car and took out a small hand-held radio. He spoke low for a moment, then nodded and put the radio back in the seat.

From across the road Dunc saw the tall man say something to the dog. The dog turned and walked away and sat down while the man opened the gate and motioned Amos inside.

Amos took one last look in Dunc's direction and disappeared into the car. The man closed the gate, stepped into the car, and drove away. Dunc sat watching the gate, wondering what he'd done and wondering what to do next.

Chapter · 8

Dunc did the only thing he could do.

He waited.

A half-hour passed, then another, then another hour.

"Two hours," he said. He was still down in the grass across the road, but he had moved several times, scratched himself, and every time he had looked over to the gate, the dog was there.

Watching.

The dog seemed to know right where Dunc was lying, and his gaze was so intent that he had forgotten to lick his chops and drool was dripping while he stared at Dunc.

"I could call the police," Dunc said, half aloud. The dog's ears perked. It looked like two notebook covers flopping up.

He's really big, Dunc thought. Not just big, but *big*. Like a car. A car that eats living things. Amos was right—he's looking at me like I was meat.

He closed his eyes and shook his head, cleared it so he could think. He needed to come up with a plan if Amos didn't come out.

Call the police—he could do that. But that would blow the whole thing.

He let his thinking free roll. Plans flew into his thoughts. Some of them were not very realistic—he thought of calling the Air Force and seeing if he could order an air strike on the dog, for instance. Or getting old really fast, getting a driver's license, borrowing his father's Buick, and aiming it at the dog.

All of them, all the plans were worthless

and he knew it, knew there was only one thing he could do, *had* to do.

He had to go in.

That's it, he thought. It was late afternoon, and it would be dark in a few hours. He looked at the dog. There it is—I have to go in.

He looked at his watch. Four o'clock. Fine. So if Amos didn't come out, he had to go in.

How long?

Well, it had been two hours. He looked at the dog once more. It was Tuesday—how about if Amos didn't come out by Friday, he would go in?

He shook his head again. Stupid.

Another hour.

There. He'd thought it and knew it was right. If Amos didn't come out in another hour, he would have to go in.

One hour.

Sixty minutes.

He started counting them, watching them flick past on his digital watch.

Time had always gone slow for him, always seemed to drag, but now it roared past. Twenty minutes were gone while he took a breath, it seemed, then another twenty and he was counting down, wondering what the dog would eat first. Probably a leg, he thought. He'd just take a leg and then come back later for anything else he wanted.

Yeah. A leg. Look at him drool, just sitting watching me drooling. I'm too young to die.

With exactly one minute to go, Dunc heard the sound of an engine and the car returned and stopped by the gate.

The same thin man got out, said something to the dog who sat down, and Amos got out.

The man opened the gate and Amos came out, stood looking up and down the street for a moment, then took his bike from next to the gate and started to ride away, the wig blowing in his face so he had trouble seeing.

The man watched for a moment until he was sure Amos was on his way, then turned the car and drove away.

As soon as he was out of sight Dunc jumped on his bike and pedaled to catch up.

"Well?"

Amos was all over the road. "My wig has moved and the hair is in my eyes—how do they ride with long hair?"

"Take it off."

They stopped and Amos took the wig off and put it in his back bike bag.

"Well?" Dunc asked.

"Well, nothing," Amos said. "I looked at so many dolls, I'm cross-eyed. You know what he's got in there?"

"No." Dunc tried not to scream. "That's what I'm trying to find out."

"Dolls," Amos said.

"Well, I figured that."

"No. I mean *dolls*. He's got dolls from all over the world. He's really a collector. He had a doll that came from some prehistoric cave in Europe. Maybe twenty thousand

45

years old. He's got another Chinese doll four thousand years old. And he's got a painting of a little girl holding the doll from way back then. I mean, it's incredible."

Amos pulled off to the side to let a car go past. "Unbelievable."

Dunc sighed. "Well, that's too bad."

"What is?"

"He sounds like a legitimate collector. I guess he isn't our man."

"I didn't say that."

"What?" Dunc had dropped in back of Amos when the car went by, and now he pulled up close next to him. "What did you say?"

"I said I didn't say he wasn't our man." Amos shook his head. "Or something. You know what I mean."

"No. I don't. Why isn't he a legitimate collector?"

Amos sat up. They were starting down a long hill, and he let his bike coast. "Oh, I think he's a collector all right—I just don't know if he's a *legitimate* collector."

"Why?"

"Well, first you have to decide on that word *legitimate*. Does that mean is he legal? Or is he just a real collector—"

"Amos."

"Do you know when you get mad, it makes your lips thin and white, the way they pinch like that?"

"Amos."

"Oh, all right. He took me all over his house, and I pretended to be interested— well, actually I guess I *was* interested. I mean that old doll, the prehistoric one, was something. He had it in a glass case, and you could just imagine a cave man sitting carving it for his kid all those years ago."

"Why is he our man?"

Amos sighed. "You should let someone tell a story when they want to tell a story. You can back these stories up, and they'll build up pressure and you'll just explode."

"All right, all right. I'm sorry. Tell it your way."

"So we're going all over the house and

47

he's showing me all these dolls, and we come to this one big glass case in a special room and it's covered with a curtain."

"The whole case?"

Amos nodded. "All around the inside. I asked him what was in the case, and he wouldn't tell me."

"It could be anything."

Amos nodded. "That's what I thought. So we'll just skip it, right?"

"You're kidding."

Amos nodded again. "We're going back, aren't we?"

"You bet."

"I wonder how hard it is to learn how to speak Rottweilerese?"

Chapter·9

"Do you know the plan—in case we get separated?" Dunc asked.

They were in Dunc's room. It was eleven at night. They were wearing black turtlenecks and jeans and had black ski masks.

"I'm wondering about this," Amos said. Dunc was rubbing camo-salve on his cheeks to knock out the light, and then he handed the tube to Amos.

"It's simple," Dunc said. "We take the back roads on our bikes. At the gate we go into Plan 1A."

"I know, I know."

"Repeat Plan 1A."

"Dunc."

"Repeat it," Dunc ordered. "It's important."

"We throw the meat to the dog."

"The whole thing," Dunc said. "Do the whole poem."

"It's hokey."

"No—it's the way the military does it. I saw it in a movie. You make a poem of the plan, and then it's easier to remember. Now do it."

Amos took a breath.

"We throw the meat to the dog
  and crawl over the log.
We pepper to the left,
  and pepper to the right.
And take very good care
  to avoid getting a bite."

"Good." Dunc nodded. "You've got it."

"It's dumb." Amos held up his can of black pepper. "This isn't going to work."

"I read that escaping slaves used to carry pepper and sprinkle it on their trail to stop the hounds from being able to follow them. It worked for them, and it will work for us."

"That thing isn't a hound," Amos said. His face was all streaks, and he looked like a clown. "It's the Devil. And he's just going to think the pepper is seasoning to make us taste better."

"Think of the reward." Dunc put his hand on the doorknob and opened it silently. "Think of Melissa," he whispered. "Now let's go—we've only got six hours before Dad and Mom wake up."

Amos held back for a moment, then followed. He hissed at Dunc's back.

"Peppered meat
is good to eat."

It took them nearly an hour to ride through the suburbs. They kept to the alleys until they were outside town, then took the road straight to the front gate. They

51

passed a few cars, one police car, but they moved off the road in plenty of time to keep from being seen.

When they arrived at the gate, they hid their bikes in the willows across the road and waited, watching.

"He's not there," Dunc said.

"He is—he's just invisible. And bullet-proof." Amos shivered, remembering. "He dripped drool when he looked at me. Dripped it *down* on my head."

"Well, I don't see him."

"Trust me. He's there. Watching us right now. Probably looking right through us. At our internal organs. Counting our organs to make sure they're all there before he— what's that?"

A sudden noise had come from the road, and Dunc sighed. "Just a cricket. Take it easy."

"I've changed my mind. Let's go home."

"Amos."

"I hate it when you say 'Amos' that way. Like you're talking to a kid."

"We *are* kids."

"I mean a real kid. A kid kid. There! What's that?"

Another sound.

"It was another cricket. Come on, let's get closer and see if we can see him."

They each had a can of pepper, and Dunc had a small pencil flashlight on a loop around his neck. Dunc also carried a plastic bag with three pounds of hamburger in it.

The plan was simple. Dunc had explained it—according to Amos—about a thousand and four times. They would throw the meat over the fence to the dog, and while he was eating it they would run to a different part of the fence, climb over, sprinkle pepper on their tracks, and make their way to the house. Amos had drawn a map of the house from memory as soon as they'd gotten back to Dunc's room. There was a set of windows in the front, and one of them had been open. If it was still open, they would go in there. If not, they would try to

53

find another way. It was a good plan, as plans went.

Except for the dog.

They couldn't find the dog.

They were close to the gate, standing against the steel grating. "If we don't find the dog," Dunc said, "we'll have to cancel."

"No problem," Amos said quietly. "I found him."

"Where is he?"

"Holding on to my thumb."

Chapter · 10

"What?"

"My thumb, you doofus," Amos almost screamed. "He's got my thumb through the gate bars here, and he's holding it."

Dunc turned, tried to see down in the darkness. "Oh yes, there he is. Why did you give him your thumb?"

"I didn't *give* him my thumb—he took it. I had my hand close to the gate, and he kind of reached through. I didn't see him in the dark. And now he won't give it back."

"Does it hurt?"

"No. He's just holding it tight. When I tried to pull it back, he grabbed tighter. Man, he's got spit all *over* my hand."

"Don't move."

"Get serious. If I leave here, I have to go without my thumb. I like my thumb. But I wish you'd do something."

"I don't know what to do. Maybe if I tap him on the nose."

"Don't get him mad!" Amos yelled.

"Shhh . . ."

"Give him the meat."

"The meat?" Dunc said. "We need that for later to distract him."

"If you don't give him the meat, I'm going to kill you."

"Wait—I've got a better idea."

"Do it soon."

Amos heard a ruffling and then a clicking sound, and suddenly the pungent odor of pepper filled the air.

Dunc sprinkled pepper through the gate bars on the Rottweiler's nose.

"Oh," Amos said, "I wish you hadn't done that."

The effect was immediate. The Rottweiler wrinkled its face, wrinkled it some more, took a great breath through its flubbery side lips, and exploded in a spray of spit and snot that covered Amos from the middle of his chest up across his face.

And he let go the thumb.

"Arrrghhh! I'm snotted, I'm snotted!"

"Don't complain." Dunc grabbed his collar and pulled him away from the gate. "He let you go, didn't he?"

"I'm snotted," Amos repeated. "He snotted me all over."

"Come on." Dunc took the plastic bag of meat and threw it over the gate. "While he's eating this, let's get in down the way."

He took off running, and Amos followed him, half dragged. Down the fence a short distance, there was a wooden bench where walkers could take a rest. It was close to the wall, and Dunc jumped on it, bounced once, and pulled himself up on top of the wall. He reached back and helped Amos up, and they dropped inside the property.

Dunc had memorized the map, and he made for the house at a good run, sprinkling pepper in back of them as he ran.

It was a huge stone house with high windows peaked like church windows. There was one yard light on over to the side, but the front and other parts of the house were dark.

"It looks spooky," Dunc said.

"Yeah. It was bad enough in daylight. It looks worse now."

"Where was that window again?"

"On the right side of the front. There— it's still open."

"Well, let's get going before the dog finds us."

"It's too late."

"What do you mean?"

"He's here. He must have swallowed the meat whole."

"Where is he? I don't see him."

"In back of me."

"He's not growling."
"He can't. His mouth is full."
"Full—of what?"
"Me. He's got me by the butt."

Chapter·11

"Lucky I've still got some pepper left."

"Couldn't we just talk to him?" Amos said. "I mean, he's not hurting me. He's just hanging on. Couldn't we talk before we do the pepper again? Couldn't we—"

It was too late. Dunc reached around to where the Rottweiler was hanging on the back of Amos's pants.

He opened the wrong hole on the pepper can, and instead of sprinkling through the small openings, he dumped half a tablespoon of pepper right on the dog's nose.

The great lips wrinkled, flubbered, wrinkled again, and the dog blew snot all over Amos's back.

"Yeeccch!"

"Run!" Dunc said. "To the window—get in the house."

They made it.

Dunc clambered in, and Amos followed.

Inside, the house was dark, pitch black. The boys stood just inside the window while Dunc found the penlight. He flicked it on once, for half a second, then off.

In the sudden glare the room looked huge, filled with hulking furniture, high shadows.

"Wrong room," Amos whispered. "It's the next one toward the back of the house."

Dunc started walking, and Amos moved next to him.

"Why are you limping?" Dunc asked.

"The dog," Amos said. "He got my shoe when I came through the window."

"Oh."

They crossed the room carefully, slowly,

and moved through the doorway into the next room.

"Flick the light," Amos said.

Dunc turned it on and off at the same time. In the quick flash they saw more furniture, couches and tables—all antiques— and in the back the glass case with the curtain.

"There," Amos said. "That's it."

They moved to the case, or tried to. Halfway across the room Amos caught a chair leg with his foot and tripped.

He went down forward, tripped Dunc on the way down. Dunc fell over onto an end table next to a large chair. The end table held a glass lamp with dangly crystals all around. The table and lamp went over with a sound loud enough to stop traffic during rush hour.

For a second, almost two, Dunc thought they'd gotten away with it.

Then they heard steps upstairs. Heavy steps. Two men, coming from two different rooms.

63

"What's that?" one of them said.

"I don't know. I think something fell downstairs. Did you let the dog in?"

"Not likely—we'd have heard long before this. I can't even leave him in the garage. Last time, he chewed one of the tires off the car."

"Well, get down there and check it out."

Dunc and Amos had been frozen in the dark on the floor, and when the speaking stopped they heard steps moving toward the top of the stairs. Dunc grabbed Amos by the collar and dragged him across the room.

There was a large chest next to the wall covered with a small Indian rug. Dunc tried it, and the lid came up. It was empty.

"Inside," he said into Amos's ear. "Hurry."

They both climbed in, and he tried to hold the rug in place as he let the lid gently down.

"It's dark," Amos whispered. "Your elbow is in my face."

"Shhhh."

They heard the light switch click on.

"Oh," the man said. "Oh, great."

He turned away, facing back up the stairs. "The window was open, and there must have been a gust. The end table and lamp blew over."

"Check the cabinet."

The boys heard steps, then the sounds of the glass case opening.

"It's all right."

"Fine. Close the window and get back to your room. We have to move the doll early tomorrow morning."

Until then everything had been going well. Or sort of well. The dog wasn't so good and the table wasn't so good, but Dunc and Amos still had luck on their side.

Until then.

At that moment the pepper container in Dunc's windbreaker pocket fell to the side. It was still open from the last sprinkle on the dog's nose.

It was almost empty. But some pepper had caught on the lip at the top, and when

it fell sideways, the pepper dropped out and
down.

Directly into Amos's nose.

It wasn't just a sneeze. The sound was
more like a machine gun going off inside the
trunk.

"Cha! Cha! Cha! Cha!"

The trunk lid opened almost immedi-
ately, and Dunc looked up to see a large
man leaning over them. He looked like a
human version of a Rottweiler.

"What are you doing in there?"

This could be going better, Dunc
thought. The man was not smiling. Amos
was upside down with his nose buried in the
corner, still sneezing.

"We're refugees," Dunc said, thinking
fast, making his voice sound foreign. "We
got lost."

"Get out of the trunk."

"Is this where we fill out our papers?"

"Get out of the trunk now. Slowly. Don't
try anything funny."

"What does this mean—funny?"

"Out."

Dunc stood and stepped out of the trunk, and Amos sat up. The man saw his face.

"You look familiar. Why is that?"

"Cha!" Amos sneezed.

"What is it, Grant?" An older man with gray hair came down the stairs.

"I found these two in the trunk."

"Oh, my—now what do we do?"

"I think," Grant said, "we have to get rid of them."

Chapter · 12

"Tell me"—Amos rubbed his nose, leaned close, and whispered in Dunc's ear—"was this part of your plan?"

"No."

"That's what I thought. This isn't good, is it?"

"Not very, no."

"Shut up, both of you," Grant said.

"Why do you want to get rid of us?" Dunc asked. "We didn't do anything."

"Exactly, Grant," the older man said. He was wearing a silk cloak with dragons up either side and silk pajamas beneath the cloak. "Why be hasty?"

Grant turned and stared at the older man. "What do you think we should do?"

"Why, the same as with any other burglar. We'll call the police and have them arrested."

"What?"

"I said—"

"I *heard* what you said. Have you forgotten about the—"

"I haven't forgotten anything. These two boys have broken into our house, and the police will come and take them away. There is nothing here that anybody cares or knows about to complicate matters."

"Oh—I see what you mean." He nodded and grabbed a phone from a nearby table and dialed the police. "Yes, officers, two boys have broken into our home. We're holding them for you. I'll have the gate open for you." He hung up and went to the wall by the front door and pushed a switch.

And Dunc thought, great, the cops will

come, and we'll tell them about the doll and—

"No," Amos said suddenly, interrupting Dunc's thought, holding up his hand, "that won't work either. See, without the doll we're just breaking and entering, but as soon as the police get here we tell them about the doll, and that gives them probable cause for a search and they'll find the doll, and there you'll be . . ." His voice trailed off, and he looked at Dunc, who was staring at him in horror. "I screwed that up, didn't I?"

"A little," Dunc said. "Well, maybe a lot. I don't think you had to tell them."

The two men looked at Amos, and the older man nodded. "Quite right. If there were such a thing as this 'doll' you're talking about. I'm sure I really don't know what you're talking about." But his eyes flicked to the case against the wall, and Dunc knew he was lying.

Dunc had been studying the case while the two men talked. It had curtains covering the glass. There didn't seem to be any real chance to escape—the men were between the boys and the window, or near it. But there was an opening toward the case. If they could break the glass, grab the doll, and run, they might be able to cause enough confusion to escape. Or at least make a mess of things until the police arrived.

"Why don't you lock our friends into the other room while I handle the situation here?" The old man's eyes went to the case once more.

Now, Dunc thought. It has to be now. Grant's hand was next to his shoulder, half an inch away, and he suddenly slammed sideways into Amos and yelled.

"The case—break the glass. Grab the doll. *Now!*"

Amos was moving before he knew why. His hand went down automatically and grabbed an ashtray off an end table by the couch, threw it overhand, and smashed the glass in on the curtain.

Dunc's hand was right in back of the ash-tray. He slid the curtain aside and grabbed the small doll from a stand in the middle of the case.

"Run!" Amos turned, fell sideways, and used his body to block into the legs of Grant, who went down like a wall falling. His hand brushed Dunc's back. The older man made one grab for him, caught his ear, and twisted it before he pulled free, and he was at the window.

It was still open.

Just enough. Out of the corner of his eye, he saw Amos just to his rear. He aimed his head at the opening and dived, at a full run, out the window.

Dunc hit the ground hard and next to him sensed a dark form, a large dark form covered with hair and snarling snot, and be-fore either he or the form could move, Amos shot through the window and landed di-rectly on the huge shadow.

Which was the Rottweiler.

There was a moment of stunned silence,

half a second, then another half, and Dunc was up, the doll in one hand, his feet moving. "Come on—run for the gate!"

Another sound, this time like somebody trying to swallow a bowling ball.

"Gackkk!" Amos said.

Dunc stopped. He was almost away, almost free, he had the doll and was almost gone, and he stopped. Amos wasn't coming. He couldn't leave without Amos. "What?"

"Ummmpphh, gackkk!" Amos said.

"We have to leave, Amos."

"Gackkk!"

It was impossible to see in the dark, but Dunc leaned down over the Rottweiler, and it seemed that he had Amos's whole head in his mouth.

The men were coming. They had gone back around through the door and were coming. Dunc threw the doll back into the bushes alongside the house and turned to meet them.

Amos was on all fours, his head and face in the dog's mouth.

74

"Oh," Dunc said, "I'm sorry. I forgot. I still have some pepper left."

"Ummmpphhh, gackkk, no!"

But it was too late. Dunc sprinkled the last of the pepper on the dog's nose. The sneeze blew Amos back four feet.

"Oh, man, I've got snot *under* my eyelids!"

"Run—" Dunc started to say, but it was too late. Grant had him by the arm, and the older man grabbed Amos.

"Where is the doll?" the old man asked.

"What doll?"

There was a small moment when Dunc thought Grant would hit him, but before he could raise his arm or Dunc could duck, sirens seemed to come from all directions, and three squad cars came down the driveway and they were surrounded by flashing red lights and police.

A large officer stopped next to Grant. "Are these the two boys?"

"Yes, officer," the older man said. "They broke into our home—"

"We were after the doll," Dunc cut in. "They have Dickens's daughter's doll—the one that was in the papers. We did some undercover work and found out they stole it and came looking for it."

The policeman sighed. "You did, eh? Have you ever heard of calling the police?"

"Yes, sir, but there wasn't time, and nobody would listen to us anyway."

"You seem familiar," the cop said. "I've seen you before, haven't I?"

Dunc was silent, but Amos—he looked like a rat drowned in spit—coughed.

"You probably remember us from when we broke that appliance stealing ring."

The cop nodded. "Oh yes, that's right. You two just about blew the whole riverfront away."

"Well, it wasn't our fault, really," Dunc said. "You see, there was this parrot—"

"Officer," the old man said, "I know it's nice to chat, but it's really very late and I have to get some rest."

"The doll," Dunc broke away from

76

Grant, who was still holding his shoulder. "They stole that doll. It's worth a lot of money, and they stole it from this nice man who drives around to shows."

"I know." The policeman nodded. "I read the reports. But I don't see a doll, do you?"

Dunc turned and moved into the bushes. "I threw it here, over here." He rummaged around where he thought he'd thrown it and couldn't find it. He tore the bushes apart but saw nothing. Then he looked up and saw the Rottweiler sitting at the edge of the bushes. A doll's leg hung out of his mouth.

"The dog's got the doll!" he said. "See?"

"How," the policeman asked, "do we get it away from him?"

"I'm out of pepper. And he won't let go— we tried to get him to let go of something before. He's stubborn. Unless . . ."

"Unless what?"

"Unless we give him a substitute. Amos," Dunc said. "Come over here by the dog and give me your arm. . . ."

Chapter · 13

"I think it worked out fairly well, don't you?" Dunc said. They were sitting on the front steps to Dunc's house. Dunc wasn't allowed to leave the boundaries of the porch until he was forty-six years old. Amos's parents were more lenient and had restricted him for only a week, with extra conditions. It had been two weeks since they had rescued the doll.

"I don't see how you can say that." Amos shook his head. "I had to dress up like a girl, was half swallowed by a Rottweiler—I *still* have spit in my ears—and I have to call home every hour on the hour for the rest of my life."

"Those two are in jail, and we got the reward, didn't we? A thousand dollars?"

"Right," Amos snorted. "And then we gave it back to the guy with the dolls so he can use it to take that motor home around and do the shows."

"It seemed the best thing to do."

"Giving away a thousand dollars *isn't* the best thing to do. Ever. I can think of many best things to do, but that isn't one of them."

"He gave us each a doll, didn't he?"

Amos looked at Dunc and didn't say anything, and Dunc nodded.

"I know, I know. It was an original set of Barbie and Ken dolls from the sixties. But he said they were collector's items and would be worth a lot of money someday."

"I gave mine to Melissa yesterday," Amos said. "It was kind of a present."

"Well there, you see? What did she do?"

"She's still laughing, but I don't know if it was the dolls or my hair. I can't get it to comb right. Dog spit makes it stand up funny. I think I had my head in that dog's mouth a little too long. I keep wanting to smell tires and chase cats." He stopped. Dunc was looking at a series of maps.

"What are you looking at?"

"There's a river rafting trip scheduled for next month. It's sponsored by the chamber of commerce, and I happen to know there are two seats still left. I was just looking at the map, and it goes through a place that looks interesting."

"What's that?"

"Down here, in the middle of the Brant Wilderness area—see here? There's a place called Dead Man's Chute. I read an article about that in the paper a month or so ago. It seems that four or five people have disappeared over the years, all right in that one place. I thought it would be something to go down there with the rafting trip—wait a minute, where are you going?"

81

Amos was halfway to the street. "Home. Forever. Good-bye."

"Melissa," Dunc said.

Amos stopped. Turned. "Melissa what?"

"She's going on the rafting trip."

Amos stared. "For sure?"

Dunc nodded. "I got it from my parents, who got it from her parents. Direct. It seems to me that sooner or later she'd *have* to talk to you, floating for a week on a raft."

Amos looked up at the sky, the trees. He sighed. "All right. When do we leave?"

Be sure to join Dunc and Amos in these other Culpepper Adventure/Mystery books:

The Case of the Dirty Bird
(Culpepper Adventure/Mystery #1)

When Dunc Culpepper and his best friend, Amos, first see the parrot in a pet store, they're not impressed—it's smelly, scruffy, and missing half its feathers. They're only slightly impressed when they learn that the parrot speaks four languages, has outlived ten of its owners, and is probably 150 years old. But when the bird starts mouthing off about buried treasure, Dunc and Amos get pretty excited—let the amateur sleuthing begin!

Culpepper's Cannon
(Culpepper Adventure/Mystery #3)

Dunc and Amos are researching the Civil War cannon that stands in the town square when they find a note inside telling them about a time portal. Entering it through the dressing room of La Petite, a women's clothing store, the boys find themselves in downtown Chatham on

March 8, 1862—the day before the historic clash between the Monitor and the Merrimack. But the Confederate soldiers they meet mistake them for Yankee spies. Will they make it back to the future in one piece?

(August 1992)

Dunc Gets Tweaked
(Culpepper Adventure/Mystery #4)

Best friends Dunc and Amos meet up with a new buddy named Lash when they enter the radical world of skateboard competition. When somebody "cops"—steals—Lash's prototype skateboard, the boys are determined to get it back. After all, Lash is about to shoot for a totally rad world's record! Along the way they learn a major lesson: *never* kiss a monkey!

(September 1992)